My Father's Shop

To Rémi

First American Edition 2006
by Kane/Miller Book Publishers, Inc.
La Jolla, California

First published in 2004 by l'école des loisirs
Copyright © 2004 l'école des loisirs, Paris

All rights reserved. For information contact:
Kane/Miller Book Publishers, Inc.
P.O. Box 8515
La Jolla, CA 92038-8515
www.kanemiller.com

Library of Congress Control Number: 2005931628
Printed and bound in China by Regent Publishing Services Ltd.
1 2 3 4 5 6 7 8 9 10

ISBN-13: 978-1-929132-99-7
ISBN-10: 1-929132-99-9

Satomi Ichikawa

My Father's Shop

Kane/Miller
BOOK PUBLISHERS

My name is Mustafa. And this is my father's shop.

He sells beautiful carpets. They come in all the colors of the world.

When foreign tourists come into the shop, my father says, "Bienvenue," and we unfold the carpets for them to see.

Then he says, "Hermoso," and adds, "Good price," which means that they are not expensive. After that, we offer the tourists mint tea.

One day, I found a little hole in a very beautiful carpet. My father was upset. "We will never sell this one! Look at that hole! What a shame!"

I didn't care about the hole. The carpet was wonderful. I loved it. "Please, Daddy, may I have this one?"

"Well," my father said, "since no one will buy it, you may have it. But you have to promise to do something for me – you must learn some foreign languages. They are very important in our trade."

"I will, I will. Thank you, Daddy." My own carpet! At last!

"Mustafa, come here," called my father a bit later.
"I will teach you some foreign words. Sit down."
"Yes, Daddy, in a minute."
"Mustafa, you promised me! We must start now.
Bienvenue means people should feel at home.
Hermoso means beautiful.
Good price means not expensive.
O cha wa ikaga desu ka? is how you offer tea."

Oh, how boring! As soon as my
father turned his back, I ran out of
the shop.

I ran through the market to show my new carpet to my friends.

Suddenly, a rooster crowed – I'm not sure where it came from – and it started to follow me. It seemed very interested in me. Maybe because of my beautiful carpet?

"Is this your new pet?" asked my friend Yacine, the mint seller.

"Is that your new rooster, Mustafa? Come on, tell him to sing," my friends called out.

"Well, I'll try…Kho Kho Hou Houuu!!" (That's how roosters crow in Morocco!)

Then the rooster echoed really loud, "Kho-kho-hou-hoûûû!"

Foreign tourists were walking by. A French boy said, "That's not how roosters sound at home! In France they say, 'Co-co-ri-co'!"

"Really?" asked a Spanish couple. "In Spain they crow, 'Qui-qui-ri-qui'!"

"How funny," the English family said. "Our roosters sing, 'Cock-a-doodle-doo'!"

"And in Japan it's, 'Koké-ko-kôôô'!"

Quickly, I ran back to my father's shop.
"Daddy! Daddy! I know lots of foreign words!
I can speak rooster in five languages!"

My father was very happy.
Not only had I learned different languages, but I
had brought all the tourists to my father's shop!